This book belongs to

_____

A READ-ALOUD STORYBOOK

Adapted by Lisa Marsoli
Illustrated by the Disney Storybook Artists

Random House 🏠 New York

Copyright © 2010 Disney Enterprises, Inc. All rights reserved. Published in the United States by Random House Children's Books, a division of Random House, Inc., 1745 Broadway, New York, NY 10019, and in Canada by Random House of Canada Limited, Toronto, in conjunction with Disney Enterprises, Inc. Random House and the colophon are registered trademarks of Random House, Inc.

Library of Congress Control Number: 2010921635

ISBN: 978-0-7364-2676-3

www.randomhouse.com/kids

Printed in the United States of America

10 9 8 7 6 5 4 3 2

Tinker Bell and her fairy friends from Pixie Hollow were on their way to bring summer to the mainland. Summer was the busiest of all the four seasons—which meant the fairies would be away from home for months instead of days.

Tinker Bell was so excited! She had heard that the fairy camp where they'd be staying was an amazing place.

Once Tink and the others arrived, the nature fairies got right to work. Vidia, a fast-flying fairy, made the summer grasses sway. Iridessa, a light fairy, bathed flowers in sunshine. Rosetta, a garden fairy, helped bees find their way to the flowers' sweet nectar. Fawn, an animal fairy, greeted birds while Silvermist, a water fairy, frolicked with pollywogs.

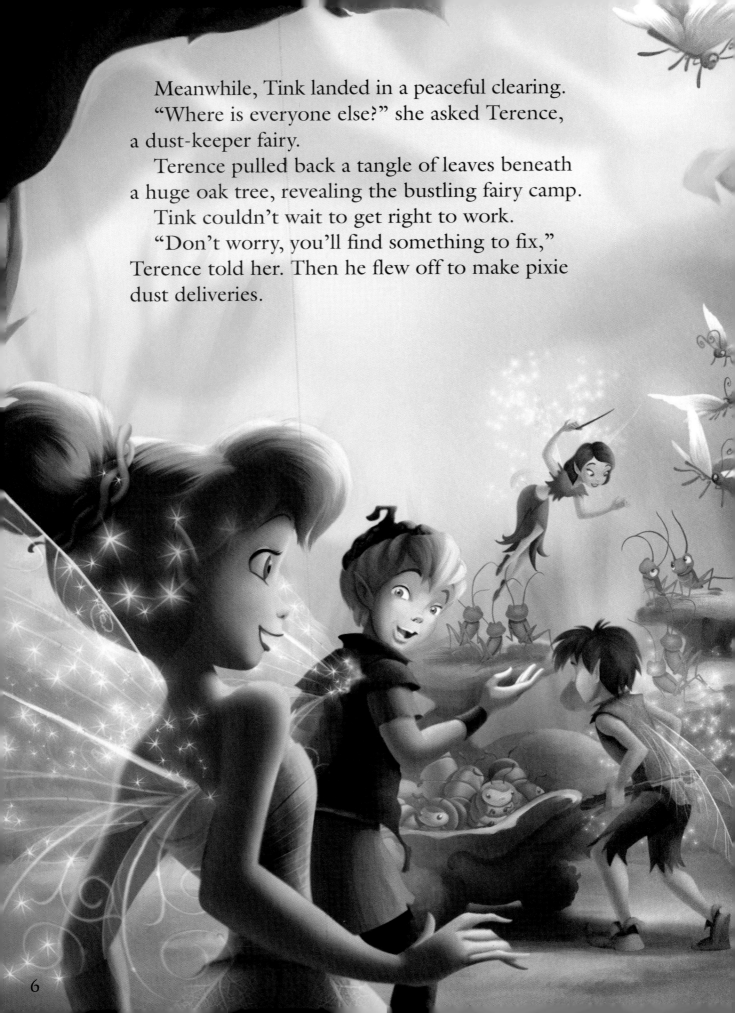

Meanwhile, Tink landed in a peaceful clearing.

"Where is everyone else?" she asked Terence, a dust-keeper fairy.

Terence pulled back a tangle of leaves beneath a huge oak tree, revealing the bustling fairy camp.

Tink couldn't wait to get right to work.

"Don't worry, you'll find something to fix," Terence told her. Then he flew off to make pixie dust deliveries.

Tink went over to a fairy who was painting stripes on bees. "How's the bee striper working? Need any tweaks?" she asked.

The bee fairy shook her head. "It's working fine, Tink," she replied.

Since there wasn't anything that needed to be repaired just yet, Tink decided to go look for Lost Things.

The other fairies reminded Tink that she needed to stay hidden from humans.

Just then, a loud *CRACK!* went through the fairy camp!
Fawn was startled and knocked over some paint she was using
to decorate butterfly wings.

Tinker Bell was very curious about what had caused the loud
noise. She flew off to find out.

It was a car! Tinker Bell had
never seen one before.

Tink followed, and watched as the car
stopped at an old house in the country.

Then she saw a little girl, her father,
and their cat get out.

"Could we have a tea party in the meadow?
Please?" Lizzy pleaded.

"Not today," Dr. Griffiths said wearily.
"I have quite a bit of work to do."

After the three had gone inside, Tink flew under the car to examine it. Suddenly, Vidia appeared. "You shouldn't be this close to the house!" she scolded.

But Tinker Bell was already poking around the engine. She found an interesting-looking lever and turned it. Outside the car, Vidia got showered with water!

Vidia was furious! Tink knew fairies couldn't fly with wet wings!

Moments later, Lizzy and her father returned to the car—and the fairies froze in fright. Luckily, the humans were busy examining a strange-looking butterfly.

"I guess that's just the way the fairies decided to paint it," Lizzy said.

"Fairies do not paint butterfly wings, because fairies are not real," Dr. Griffiths insisted as he captured the creature with a net.

Meanwhile, Lizzy was pulling a fairy house out of the trunk of the car. She hoped a real fairy would come to live in her miniature house one day. Lizzy invited her father to help her set it up in the meadow, but—as usual—he was too busy. He had to get ready for a meeting he was having at the museum the next day.

When the humans had left, Tinker Bell apologized to Vidia for getting her wet.

"Maybe if you spent less time causing disasters," Vidia snapped, "you wouldn't have to help everybody so much."

The pair set off together into the meadow, where they soon spotted Lizzy's fairy house.

Tink flew over to investigate.

"Tinker Bell, we're not supposed to go near human houses!" warned Vidia.

"Human houses are a lot bigger," Tink replied. She went inside and looked around, delighted by the tiny furnishings. "It's perfectly safe."

"Oh, really?" asked Vidia. She stepped outside and whipped up a gust of wind that slammed the door shut.

Tink didn't mind. She was having fun exploring.

Suddenly, Vidia saw Lizzy approaching in the distance. She pulled on the door to let Tink out—but it was jammed shut!

"Tink, someone's coming!" cried Vidia. "Get out of there!"

Tink ignored her. She was sure Vidia was just trying to scare her.

Vidia hid, watching as Lizzy got closer. "Oh, no! What have I done?" she cried as the little girl peeked into the house.

"A . . . a . . . a fairy . . . ," Lizzy whispered.

Tinker Bell saw Lizzy's huge eye staring at
her through the window. It was terrifying! Lizzy
snatched up the fairy house and raced back home.
Vidia followed at a safe distance.

Dr. Griffiths was busy studying the butterfly he
had captured earlier.

"Now, dear," Dr. Griffiths said. "What did you
want me to see?"

"Um, never mind . . . ," Lizzy answered. She
worried that her father might try to study the fairy
the way he was studying the butterfly.

Up in her room, Lizzy took the roof off the fairy house, and *ZIP!* Tinker Bell darted out.

Vidia watched through the window as Mr. Twitches pounced. Tinker Bell was in more danger than Vidia had thought!

Lizzy scooped Tinker Bell out of the way and put her in a birdcage for safekeeping.

"Bad cat! No, no, no!" cried Lizzy.

Vidia raced back to the fairy camp to get help, but a storm had begun.

"We can't fly in the rain," Fawn reminded her. "And the meadow's already flooded!"

Clank and Bobble had the answer: They would build a boat!

Back at the house, Lizzy let Tinker Bell out of the cage and showed off her collection of fairy artwork. But as Lizzy described what was going on in each picture, Tink realized that the little girl had her fairy facts all wrong!

Tink interrupted, but all Lizzy heard was a jingling sound. "So that's how fairies speak!" she exclaimed.

Tink went over to the fairy house and started repairing the door.

"Why, you're quite the little tinker, aren't you?" asked Lizzy.

Tink pointed to herself, then rang the house's fairy bell.

"Tinker Bell!" Lizzy cried. "What a lovely name!"

Just then, Dr. Griffiths came upstairs to deal with some leaks in the old house's ceilings.

"Lizzy," he said, "it sounds like you're talking to . . . a fairy?"

Tinker Bell hid while Lizzy quickly held up a fairy drawing. "Oh, yes, but she's make-believe," the little girl replied.

"Quite right," her father said. "I would like to see you spending less time in the fantasy world and more time in the real world. This summer you have an excellent opportunity to learn all sorts of wonderful things. Here is a blank field journal. I'm sure you'll be able to fill it with your own scientific research."

Satisfied, her father went back to his task.

Tinker Bell came out of hiding. She was ready to go home, but a rainstorm had begun!

"You can stay with me until it stops," suggested Lizzy. "You can teach me more about fairies!"

Tinker Bell had an idea. She gathered together some art supplies, then opened the blank field journal.

Lizzy asked her questions about being a fairy, and Tinker Bell acted out the answers.

Soon Tink and Lizzy had filled the journal!

Meanwhile, Tinker Bell's friends were having a rough voyage in their homemade boat. In fact, they were headed straight for a waterfall!

After a wild ride, the boat crashed on the shore. The fairies were safe—but their boat was in pieces.

"I guess our sailing days are over," said Bobble.

Now that Lizzy's fairy field journal was complete and the rain was slowing down, it was time for Tink to go find her friends. Tinker Bell was sad about leaving, but excited to get back to the fairy camp.

"Good-bye, Tinker Bell," Lizzy said. "I'll never forget you."

But when Tinker Bell flew past the office window, she saw Lizzy inside. It was obvious the little girl wanted her father to look at her journal—but he was too busy trying to fix all the leaks in the house.

Tink realized she couldn't leave just yet. She had to find a way to help Lizzy and her father spend more time together.

Lizzy went back to her room, feeling sad. Suddenly, Tink appeared!

"You came back!" Lizzy exclaimed. She was overjoyed to see her new friend again!

Meanwhile, the other fairies were on foot, continuing their mission to find Tink. Vidia finally spotted the road that led to Lizzy's house. Everyone crossed the road safely except Vidia. She got stuck in the mud! Silvermist, Fawn, Rosetta, and Iridessa grabbed on to Vidia and pulled—but they couldn't budge her.

Then, suddenly, the fairies saw headlights coming toward them in the rain!

Iridessa held up her hand and bounced the headlight beams back toward the car. The driver stopped and got out. "Is somebody out there?" he asked.

The fairies reached out for his shoelace and held on tight. When the driver turned to leave, he pulled them all out of the mud!

After a fun evening of playing with Tink, and a yummy tea party, Lizzy fell asleep. Tink peeked into the hallway and saw Dr. Griffiths give up and head to bed himself as even more drips fell from the ceiling.

That gave Tinker Bell an idea. If she could help Dr. Griffiths with the house repairs, he would have more time to spend with Lizzy!

Tinker Bell found a hole in the ceiling and flew up into the attic. The musty old place was filled with crates and boxes—and leaks!

She searched the attic until she had all the parts she needed. In no time at all, she had invented a system to take the water from the leaks and send it back outside.

Tinker Bell flew down into the office to make sure her repairs had worked.

She couldn't help noticing the butterfly fluttering in a jar on the desk. It made Tink feel terrible to see the poor creature trapped and helpless.

By the time Tink was done taking care of the leaks, it was morning.

Dr. Griffiths came by to check on his daughter. "All the leaks seem to have stopped," he told her. "It's as if they mended themselves."

When Dr. Griffiths left the room, Tink picked up the field journal. She encouraged Lizzy to take it to her father.

"I *would* like to show him this," Lizzy said. "He has so much to learn about fairies."

But when Lizzy got downstairs, her father was very upset. "The butterfly is gone," he announced. "I was going to present it at the museum tonight. I didn't let it go, and since there is no one else in this house, it must have been you."

"I didn't," replied Lizzy. "It must have been . . ."

Tinker Bell started toward the office, but Lizzy waved her away.

"It must have been who?" Dr. Griffiths asked.

"I could tell you, Father," Lizzy declared, "but you wouldn't believe me."

"Very well," Dr. Griffiths said, "off to your room. I'm very disappointed in you."

In the woods nearby, Tinker Bell's friends made their way silently through the rain.

"I was just thinking, if Tink were here," said Silvermist, "how *not* quiet it would be right now. I really miss her."

"Tinker Bell getting trapped is all my fault," Vidia admitted. "I'm so sorry."

To Vidia's surprise, the other fairies weren't upset with her.

"Tinker Bell can get into plenty of trouble by herself," Rosetta declared.

The fairies joined hands and vowed to work together to save Tink.

Meanwhile, Tinker Bell was trying to make Lizzy feel better. "I wish I were a fairy just like you," Lizzy told Tink. "Then I could fly around with the other fairies all the time."

Tink knew how to make Lizzy's wish come true: pixie dust!

While Lizzy was being a pretend fairy upstairs, lots of real fairies were slipping into the kitchen downstairs to rescue Tink!

They didn't get very far, though. Mr. Twitches was blocking their way!

Vidia had an idea. She shot a stream of pixie dust at a plate, which began to hover in the air. The others joined in, sprinkling the magic dust on dishes and silverware. Now the fairies hurried across their flying bridge to reach the stairs—but Mr. Twitches was right behind them.

"You know where Tink is," Rosetta told Vidia. "You go. We'll take care of the cat."

At the same time, Dr. Griffiths could hear strange noises coming from Lizzy's room.

"What's going on in here?" he demanded. "Look at this room! How did you get footprints on the ceiling? The truth this time."

"Well, I . . . ," began Lizzy. "I was flying. My fairy showed me how."

"You've got to stop this nonsense!" insisted Dr. Griffiths.
Just then, Vidia sneaked into the room, but he didn't see her.
"You will never convince me that fairies exist!" he added.
Tinker Bell couldn't stand it any longer. She flew out of hiding
and hovered directly in front of his face!

"It can't be!" Lizzy's father cried. He stared at Tink in wonder. "This is going to be the discovery of the century!"

Vidia saw him raise a glass jar. "Watch out!" she warned. Now that her wings were dry, she was able to fly over and knock Tink out of the way.

SLAM! The jar came down on Vidia instead.

I must get this to the museum right away." declared Dr. Griffiths.

"Father, you can't do this!" cried Lizzy—but it was no use.

Dr. Griffiths ran out of the house, jumped into his car, and drove off to the city.

When the other fairies arrived, Tink told them that Vidia was in danger. "We have to hurry and rescue her!" she cried.

It was still raining, though. The fairies wouldn't be able to fly.

"*We* can't fly," said Tink, "but I think I know somebody who can."

The fairies swirled around Lizzy and showered her with pixie dust.

"All aboard!" cried Tinker Bell.

The fairies tucked themselves into Lizzy's raincoat, and off she flew down the road that led to the city.

Shortly after nightfall, the magnificent streets of London came into view.

"There he is!" cried Lizzy as she spotted her father's car.
Tinker Bell flew down and bravely darted into the engine.
After some quick tinkering, the car sputtered and stopped.

Dr. Griffiths jumped out and raced off toward the museum
on foot. Tinker Bell—and Lizzy—were right behind him.

"Father!" Lizzy called.

Dr. Griffiths turned to see his daughter flying toward him.
"Lizzy . . . you're . . . flying!

"But I don't understand," Dr. Griffiths continued.

"You don't have to understand," Lizzy told her father.

Dr. Griffiths looked at all the tiny magical fairies hovering around him. His eyes filled with wonder. "I just need to believe," he said. He handed the jar to Lizzy. Seconds later, Vidia was reunited with her relieved and grateful friends.

Then everyone—including Dr. Griffiths—received a generous sprinkling of pixie dust and flew back to the country.

The next day, everyone enjoyed a lovely tea party in the meadow.

"Isn't this pleasant, Father?" asked Lizzy.

"I can't imagine anything better," Dr. Griffiths answered. "Although flying over London Bridge is a close second."

Tink and Vidia sat together, sipping their tea. Not only did they know each other better now—but they had actually become good friends!

A little while later, everyone settled in to hear Dr. Griffiths read from Lizzy's fairy field journal.

Just then, Terence returned from his pixie dust deliveries. "Well," he said to Tinker Bell, "you found something to fix after all."

Tink looked at Lizzy snuggled close to her father.

"I guess I did," she replied with a satisfied smile.